First American Edition 2017
Kane Miller, A Division of EDC Publishing

Text copyright © Lesley Gibbes, 2016
Illustrations copyright © Stephen Michael King, 2016
First published by Allen & Unwin Pty Ltd, Sydney, Australia

For information contact:
Kane Miller, A Division of EDC Publishing
PO Box 470663
Tulsa, OK 74147-0663
www.kanemiller.com
www.edcpub.com
www.usbornebooksandmore.com

Library of Congress Control Number: 2016944301

Printed in the United States of America
2 3 4 5 6 7 8 9 10
ISBN: 978-1-61067-614-4

FiZZ
and the SHOW DOG JEWEL THIEF

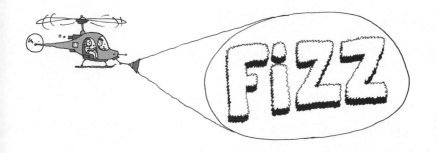

BOOK 3

For Rodney, Austin and Georgia. L.G.

For Twiggy. S.M.K.

Fizz

and the
SHOW DOG
JEWEL THIEF

LESLEY
GIBBES

ILLUSTRATED BY
STEPHEN
MICHAEL
KING

Kane Miller
A DIVISION OF EDC PUBLISHING

Fizz

Razor

Remi Razzle

Sheridan

Miss Sparkles

Fizz's mother

CONTENTS

With special thanks to Margaret Connolly, Sue Flockhart, Erica Wagner, Stephen Michael King and Trish Hayes.

L.G.

Chapter 1

The First Case

"I did it! I'm really here!" barked Fizz, as he stood outside Sunnyvale City Police Station on his first day of work. His heart was beating fast. This was the day he'd been dreaming of. This was the day he would be a real undercover police dog.

"Too chicken to go in, Powder Puff? Little loser!" sneered Amadeus, bounding up the stairs. "Why don't you go back to the dog shows where you belong? Leave the police work to the big boys."

Amadeus flicked his back paws at Fizz, then burst through the double doors into the busy police station. He didn't think a small, fluffy dog like Fizz could be a bold undercover police dog.

Fizz took a deep breath then stepped inside. He was determined to do his best, and to prove Amadeus wrong.

Sunnyvale City Police Station was buzzing with activity. Sergeant Stern appeared from the crowd in his smart blue uniform. He marched over to Fizz and Amadeus.

"Welcome to Sunnyvale City Police Station," he said proudly. "And congratulations on passing your training at the Blue Haven Police Academy for Dogs. I'm expecting big things from my two Top Dog graduates."

Fizz puffed out his chest.

He was raring to begin.

"This way, boys," said Sergeant Stern, leading Fizz and Amadeus down a corridor to his office. "You have a case to solve."

Fizz and Amadeus sat in front of Sergeant Stern's desk. Fizz wondered what their first case might be.

"Your job," said Sergeant Stern, opening a bulging police file, "is to catch the Show Dog Jewel Thief."

Yes! thought Fizz. This was just the case he needed to show Amadeus how clever he could be.

"Fizz, I'm sending you deep undercover… as a show dog contestant at the Pemberley Show Dog Trials."

"What did I tell you, Miss Fluffy Puppy," sniggered Amadeus into Fizz's ear. "You're just a little show dog!"

Fizz's tail dropped. Convincing Amadeus he was smart and fearless wasn't going to be easy, especially when he was groomed as a show dog. He concentrated on the Sergeant.

"The Show Dog Jewel Thief has stolen the winner's tiara at the last three championships," said Sergeant Stern. "Your job is to catch the jewel thief before he can steal this one."

He held up a photograph of a glittering tiara.

"The Pemberley Tiara is the most expensive tiara on the show dog circuit. I'm sure the jewel thief is going to strike again. My hunch is he's a show dog contestant. That's why I want an undercover police dog on the job."

Sergeant Stern looked at Amadeus.

"Amadeus, you will be on general patrol at the trials, looking for anything suspicious. I want both of you to stay alert. The Show Dog Jewel Thief knows a few tricks. He likes to create a diversion — like cutting the lights or activating the fire alarm — before he steals the tiara during the crowning ceremony. Your job is to catch the jewel thief red-handed before he makes his escape. Can I count on you?" asked Sergeant Stern.

"You just play the fluffy show dog, Powder Puff," whispered Amadeus. "I'll be the one who catches the jewel thief, not you. Got it?"

"Well and good," said Sergeant Stern. "The Pemberley Show Dog Trial starts today."

Chapter 2

The Makeover

Sergeant Stern drove Fizz and Amadeus to Gorgeous Groomers Show Dog Salon.

"You'll need to look the part as a show dog contestant," he said to Fizz, opening the rear door of the police paddy wagon.

"So I've booked you in with the groomers."

"You're going to look gorgeous, Powder Puff!" Amadeus jumped onto the sidewalk beside Fizz.

"And just to be sure you pull off the look, I've recruited some expert help," said Sergeant Stern, opening the salon door.

The salon smelled of frangipani talcum powder and was decorated in pink-and-white hearts.

"Surprise!" said a familiar voice.

"Mom?" said Fizz, blinking.

"That's right, sugarplum," said Fizz's mother, rushing to greet him. "Sergeant Stern told me he wants you to be in the Pemberley Show. I'm so excited, my little Fizz competing in his very first show dog competition. You're going to look sensational when Sheridan's finished with you!"

Fizz gulped as a willowy man with pink hair swept across the salon waving a pair of dog clippers.

"Welcome, darlings," he said, looking from Fizz to Amadeus. "So who's the lucky dog getting the Sheridan treatment today?"

"Miss Fluffy!" said Amadeus, pushing Fizz forward. "He can't wait for his makeover."

11

"Up you come, darling," said Sheridan, patting a pink salon chair.

Amadeus howled with laughter.

"I'm not actually competing," explained Fizz, looking at his reflection in a heart-shaped mirror. "I just have to blend in with the other show dogs to catch the jewel thief."

"The jewel thief?" exclaimed Sheridan, "No one knows who the jewel thief is – or how he's getting the tiaras out. The police searched every contestant's bag last time, but they found nothing."

Sergeant Stern nodded.

"However, we did find a clue from each crime scene," said Sergeant Stern. "A glass bead, a white hair and a patch of spilled talcum powder that later mysteriously disappeared off the stage."

Fizz thought about the clues as Sheridan teased and bunched his fur into various hairstyles.

"Well, if you're going to be a show dog contestant, you absolutely must have a show dog name," said Sheridan.

"He looks like a Snookums to me," sniggered Amadeus.

"Oh no," said Fizz's mother. "I've had Fizz's show dog name picked out since he was a pup. It's Angel!"

Fizz's ears sagged.

"Oh, Angel sounds perfect," said Sheridan, pulling Fizz's hair into a high bouffant. "So what do you think, curly or straight?"

"I've always wanted to see Fizz in curls," said Fizz's mother, sighing.

"Definitely curls," grinned Amadeus, "and bows…big pink ones."

"Curls and bows it is," said Sheridan, reaching for a roll of pink sparkly ribbon and a box of hot rollers.

Fizz gave Sergeant Stern a look that said, "Do I *have* to?"

"You're going to be fine, Fizz. And you won't be alone. There'll be another undercover police dog on the job too."

Fizz wondered who it could be.

"Just keep your eyes peeled and use what you learned at the academy. I'm counting on you to catch the Show Dog Jewel Thief and solve your first case."

Fizz hoped he wouldn't let Sergeant Stern down.

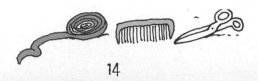

Chapter 3
The Gang's All Here!

"Stand up straight, sugarplum. I mean, Angel," said Fizz's mother, at the door to the Pemberley Show Dog Hall. "A winning show dog knows the judges are always watching."

Fizz couldn't believe his eyes. The Pemberley Show Dog Hall was glittering and grand and crowded with exotic show dogs in sparkling costumes. In the center of the hall was a spectacular competition arena that glowed under the lights of six crystal chandeliers. Beside the arena was a magnificent stage, and sitting on a pedestal, center stage, was the dazzling Pemberley Tiara.

Fizz was so relieved that he didn't have to compete.

"Right, sugarplum," said Fizz's mother, weaving through the elegant chairs and coffee tables that surrounded the arena. "Leave everything to me. I'll check that your costume bag has arrived and find a chair by the arena. And I'll enter you in the competition just in case you change your mind."

"What? *No!* Mom…" Fizz said, but his mother had already dashed off to the registration table at the back of the hall.

Fizz lowered his eyes.

Somewhere amongst the crowd of show dogs was the Show Dog Jewel Thief. Fizz set to work sniffing around the hall, searching for clues.

"Oh, *curls*," said a contestant in a sparkling red skirt. "That's so last season!"

Fizz looked up. It was Remi Razzle! She winked at Fizz.

"Hi, I'm *Sequin*," she said.

Fizz laughed. "I'm *Angel*," he said, shaking his bows and curls so they bounced like springs. "What are you doing here?"

"Undercover to catch the Show Dog Jewel Thief," whispered Remi, nodding at the tiara.

"Oh, good. Me too," said Fizz. "Let's team up and search the hall together."

"Excuse me, madam," said a chocolate-brown Labrador in a trainee rescue dog coat.

Fizz spun around. It was Benny!

"Benny, it's me, Fizz!" he said, shaking the curls off his face.

"Fizz? You look like a *girl*!"

"It's a disguise," said Fizz, rolling his eyes. "I'm undercover with Remi. We're here to catch the Show Dog Jewel Thief. What are you doing?"

"The Rescue Squad's on standby in case there's another commotion," said Benny, bouncing up and down enthusiastically. "Have you worked out who the jewel thief is yet?"

"There are so many dogs, it could be anyone," said Remi, shaking her head.

"Let's start with the clues," said Fizz. "Sergeant Stern said the police found three. The first clue was a white hair."

"But lots of dogs have white hair," said Remi, scanning the hall. "That means heaps of suspects."

"There was a glass bead too," said Fizz. "*And* the mysterious disappearance of a patch of spilled talcum powder."

"So we're looking for a white-haired, bead-wearing dog with a cleaning fetish!" laughed Remi.

"Okay," said Fizz. "The clues aren't much help."

Fizz, Remi and Benny searched the hall together as more dogs arrived for the competition.

"Out of my way!" said a cranky show dog mom, wearing a shiny beaded collar. "My Brittney's coming through."

Who's Brittney? thought Fizz.

A perfectly clipped miniature poodle, in an emerald tutu and matching emerald tiara, strutted towards him.

"Brittney's a champion," said Benny. "She's won the last three show dog competitions."

Brittney stopped in front of Fizz.

"How embarrassing," she said, raising her nose at Fizz's bows and curls. "Hasn't anyone told you pink's *not* your color?"

Brittney tossed her head rudely and walked on, followed by an entourage of groomers and attendants.

"What was that about?" asked Fizz.

"That's just trash talk to put you off your game," said Benny. "She thinks you might win. You'd better watch out for her. She sabotaged Jemarcus's costume at the last competition."

"Which one's Jemarcus?" asked Fizz, becoming interested.

"Oh, you can't miss him," said Benny, bouncing up and down like a pogo stick. "He's a mop dog. He's at the registration table entering the competition."

A loud gasp erupted from the crowd as an enormous komondor entered the hall. There were beads all through his coat, and an emerald-green medallion around his neck. His dreadlocked hair swept the floor like a giant mop.

"Oh," said Benny, looking at the komondor. "*That's* Jemarcus. I could have sworn he was just at the registration table. I must be more nervous than I thought."

"What's with the gasping?" asked Remi.

"Jemarcus is wearing emerald green," whispered Benny. "Everyone knows emerald is Brittney's signature color. No one else would dare wear it. He's done that on purpose to upset her."

Fizz looked up as Jemarcus swept past.

"Cool curls, babe," he said, winking at Fizz.

Benny grinned. "I told you, you look like a girl."

Fizz swatted Benny with the bow on his tail.

"What else do we know about the jewel thief?" asked Fizz, quickly changing the subject.

"We know he steals the tiara during the crowning ceremony," said Remi.

"Exactly," said Fizz. "The jewel thief would have to be on the stage to do that. That means we have to be on the stage, too, if we want to catch him red-handed."

"But how?" asked Remi, noting the two guard dogs by the stairs to the stage. "The only dogs allowed on the stage during the crowning ceremony are the top six finalists."

"So," said Fizz, "there's only one way to be on the stage to catch the Show Dog Jewel Thief when he steals the tiara. *We* have to compete *and* win!"

An official voice boomed over the loud-speaker.

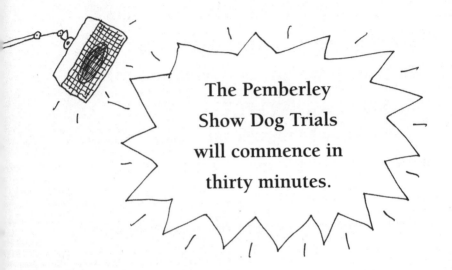

The Pemberley Show Dog Trials will commence in thirty minutes.

Fizz groaned.

"What's wrong?" asked Remi.

"I've got to tell Mom!"

Chapter 4
The Costume

"I can't believe it. I just can't believe it," gushed Fizz's mother, fussing over the bow on his tail. "My Fizz is competing in the biggest show dog competition of the year. And look," Fizz's mother grinned at Remi, "you have a girlfriend already! Well I'm not surprised. You are a catch, just like your father!"

Remi giggled.

"Mom, this is Remi," said Fizz, blushing under his fur. "She's an undercover police dog, like me. We both have to compete if we're going to be on the stage to catch the jewel thief. Do you think you can help us get to the top six?"

"Well, of course I can, sugarplum!" said Fizz's mother, beaming. "I am a show dog mom after all." She examined them closely. "We're going to have to work on your costumes," she said. "Today's Fashion Show is fancy dress."

Fizz's mother searched through a large costume bag laid out on a crimson sofa.

"I had your father's old costumes and diamond collar packed just in case."

Fizz's eyes boggled at the sparkling collar. "Mom, there's a jewel thief on the loose. Dad's collar might get stolen!"

"Don't worry, sugarplum. I won't let the collar out of my sight." She rummaged through the bag, and pulled out a frilly pink bonnet and a red heart locket.

"The bonnet is for you, Fizz," she said. "You're going as Little Bo Peep. And Remi can wear the heart locket. She'll be the Queen of Hearts."

An attendant put the locket around Remi's neck. He put the bonnet on Fizz's head and tied an enormous pink bow under Fizz's chin.

"Adorable!" said Fizz's mother.

"Ridiculous," said Fizz.

"Well, it could be worse," said Remi, tilting her head to a sponsor's poster at the back of the hall.

Fizz saw a giant picture of Bruno with a pile of pink bubbles on his head – advertising deodorant shampoo for smelly dogs!

Fizz laughed. It definitely could be worse!

"Now," said Fizz's mother, suddenly serious, "the other show dogs will try to undermine you at every turn. So be alert. Watch your feet for any tripping hazards and make sure you check your costume before you enter the arena."

"You make it sound like a battlefield," said Remi. She could see Brittney being groomed by her entourage of helpers.

"This is the biggest show dog event on the calendar. Of course it's a battlefield!" said Fizz's mother, straightening Fizz's bonnet.

"So how can we possibly win?" asked Fizz.

"To place well at the Fashion Show you'll need more than a great costume. What you need is a signature move. Your father's was a high kick leap and a cheeky wink."

An announcement blared across the hall.

"Would all show dog competitors please assemble in the holding area. The Fashion Show is about to begin."

"You'll need a score of eight or more to make it to the next round," said Fizz's mother. "You're going to be fantastic, sugarplum!"

Chapter 5

The Fashion Show

"Welcome to the Pemberley Show Dog Trials." An elegant lady, in a shimmering ball gown, held a microphone in the center of the arena. "My name is Miss Sparkles and I am your host today. Would you please welcome our judges."

Fizz and Remi watched from the crowded holding area as three judges appeared. They took their positions at a long table in the middle of the arena.

"Ready?" asked Remi.

"Ready?" said Fizz. "My legs are trembling like a nervous Chihuahua."

"Move it, princess," said Brittney, bumping Fizz aside. "Don't go getting any ideas, sweetie. That tiara is mine!"

Brittney glared at Fizz, then strutted onto the arena as Miss Sparkles announced her.

"That Brittney's a piece of work," said Remi. "She wants the tiara so bad anyone would think *she* was the jewel thief!"

Brittney paraded around the arena as Little Miss Muffet, dressed in an emerald skirt with a spider motif and a bowl of curds and whey nestled inside the tiara on her head. She struck an exotic pose in front of the judges and scored a nine.

Miss Sparkles announced the next contestant. It was Jemarcus.

"This is the last competition for Jemarcus," said Miss Sparkles. "He's retiring today to travel the world with his twin brother."

35

Jemarcus was in a superhero costume, with a medallion and sparkling green cape. He glided around the arena and stopped in front of the judges… then chased his tail until he was a blur of sparkling green.

"That's his signature move," said a Pekinese to Fizz.

The judges held up their scorecards. Jemarcus had scored a nine!

Fizz's stomach fluttered with nerves. He'd need a signature move too if he was going to impress the judges.

"Our next contestant is Sequin," announced Miss Sparkles.

"Wish me luck," said Remi.

Fizz crossed his paws.

Remi high stepped around
the arena then spun in front of
the judges, swishing her tail in
a dazzling full circle. She scored
an eight.

"Too chicken to compete, Powder Puff?"
said a gruff voice beside Fizz.

It was Amadeus on patrol.

"Can't say I blame you, looking like
that! I've already found two leads and put
someone on the inside." Amadeus nodded
at one of the guard dogs on the stage stairs.
It was Razor! "You'll never make it onto the
stage, loser!" he said, swatting Fizz's bonnet
with his tail before bounding away.

Fizz crumpled. Amadeus was right. Remi was a circus dog, and the other show dogs had been competing since they were pups. This was Fizz's very first competition. He watched the other entrants perform until Miss Sparkles finally announced: "Our last contestant is Angel."

An excited squeal erupted from the crowd. It was Fizz's mother.

Fizz was hot and clammy. He needed a signature move, but what to do?

"Oh, sorry," said Brittney, tugging the bow on Fizz's tail, "did I do that?"

Brittney had unraveled the bow completely. Fizz looked like a mess!

Miss Sparkles called his name again.

"What a shame," said Brittney, smirking. "It's too late to fix your costume now."

"This is the last call for Angel," said Miss Sparkles, looking worried. Fizz felt panicky. He needed help.

Remi swooped in and yanked off the loose ribbon.

"Go," she said, pushing Fizz forward.

The crowd hushed as Fizz skidded onto the arena.

He froze under the spotlight.

"Look, he's got stage fright," howled Amadeus from the sideline.

"Come on, Angel, you can do it!" cheered Benny, bouncing at the edge of the arena.

Signature move, thought Fizz. *A signature move…*

Suddenly, he had an idea. Fizz raised himself onto his tiptoes and pranced around the arena with his curls and bonnet bouncing.

The crowd sighed. Fizz was entrancing, as cute as pie… but it wasn't enough. He needed something else. Something spectacular. He stopped in front of the judges and shook his fur until his curls exploded into a giant Afro. He was a total ball of fur!

The judges gasped in surprise. Fizz held his breath as his fur stood on end. He scored a ten!

"My collar," yelped Fizz's mother from the crowd. "Someone's stolen my diamond collar!"

Fizz's skin prickled with goose bumps.

"The jewel thief is here!"

HELP!

Chapter 6

The First Clue

"I only left our bag for a minute," said Fizz's mother. The costume bag was wide-open. "I just had to see you compete. When I came back the collar was *gone*."

Fizz gave his mother a comforting nuzzle. "Do you remember anything suspicious, Mom?"

"Nothing."

"Is it really gone?" said Remi.

Fizz searched through the bag.

"Yes, the collar's gone. But I've found something else!"

"Is it a hair?" asked Remi.

"No," said Fizz. "It's an emerald."

Fizz's eyes flashed. "Remi, there are only two dogs wearing emerald jewels today: Brittney and Jemarcus. We've narrowed our suspects to two dogs!"

Remi danced in a full circle, then suddenly stopped. "But Brittney or Jemarcus couldn't have stolen the diamond collar if they were competing," she said.

Fizz slumped. Remi was right. Brittney or Jemarcus couldn't have stolen the collar if they were in the Fashion Show. It was impossible. No one can be in two places at once.

Fizz paced back and forth in front of his costume bag.

"Sergeant Stern said the jewel thief caused a diversion before each of the winning tiaras were stolen," said Fizz. "The jewel thief can't steal the tiara *and* cause a diversion at the same time."

Fizz stopped in his tracks. He couldn't believe he hadn't thought of it before. "We're not looking for *one* jewel thief, Remi. We're looking for *two*!"

"You mean the jewel thief has an accomplice," said Remi, her eyes widening.

"The accomplice creates the diversion while the jewel thief steals the tiara," said Fizz, wagging his tail. "The jewel thief has to be Brittney. Jemarcus is here alone!"

"And she has white hair," said Remi, recalling Sergeant Stern's clues.

"And Brittney's mother wears a beaded glass collar," said Fizz.

"The clues fit!" said Remi.

"Brittney and her mother are the jewel thieves for sure!" said Fizz. "But we don't have enough evidence to arrest them. To do that, we'll have to catch them red-handed with the tiara during the crowning ceremony!"

The loud speaker crackled.

Would all qualifying dogs please assemble in the holding area for the Talent Quest.

Fizz shook off his bonnet.

"Let's go," he said. "We've got a Talent Quest to win!"

Chapter 7

The Talent Quest

"What are we going to do?" said Fizz, his nose suddenly dry. "We haven't had time to rehearse an item for the Talent Quest. If we don't score nine or more we'll be out of the competition."

Remi's eyes brightened. "I could do my tumble routine. It was a big hit at the circus. What will you do, Fizz?"

Fizz couldn't think of anything he could do.

Benny bounded over to wish them luck.

"I've just finished a safety check of the electrical mains closet," he said. "Everything in there smelled of bacon." His stomach rumbled loudly. "Speaking of bacon," said Benny, licking his chops, "Jemarcus is a mess. He spilled a whole bowl of bacon and gravy down his chin. The judges will mark him down for sure!"

At that very
moment Jemarcus
swished past. He
was wearing a green
baseball cap and

bandanna and his emerald medallion.

"So, you got the gravy stain out all
right?" said Benny, noting Jemarcus's
spotless chin.

"What you talking about, man?" said
Jemarcus.

"The gravy mess on your chin," said
Benny. "I saw you just now in the canteen."

"You got the wrong dog, man. I don't
eat and compete. You lose points for food
stains," said Jemarcus.

Benny's tail sagged as he watched Jemarcus glide over to the holding area. "I'll see you guys later," he said.

"Poor Benny," said Remi. "He's so rattled about the jewel thief, he's seeing Jemarcus everywhere. Anyone would think he's seeing double."

Miss Sparkles tapped her microphone. The Talent Quest was about to begin. "Ready, everyone? Our first contestant is Jemarcus," said Miss Sparkles, "with a performance on his skateboard."

Music pumped as Jemarcus zipped around the arena and up onto the stage on his shimmering green skateboard. His dreadlocks swung in all directions, revealing a glittering undercoat that flashed as it caught the light. The crowd cheered for Jemarcus!

"A dazzling performance," said Miss Sparkles.

"Wow!" said Remi, squinting. "How did he get his coat to sparkle like that? It looked like diamonds."

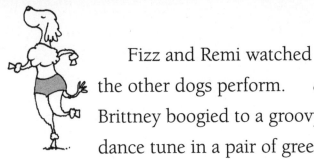

Fizz and Remi watched the other dogs perform. Brittney boogied to a groovy dance tune in a pair of green hot pants, a miniature whippet jumped through a tricky arrangement of hoops, and a beagle raced around the arena balancing a liver treat on his nose.

Remi was up next. She performed her incredible tumbling act and received a standing ovation and a score of nine!

Fizz was sweating because he still didn't know what to do.

"Our final contestant is Angel," said Miss Sparkles.

Fizz's legs wobbled like jelly.

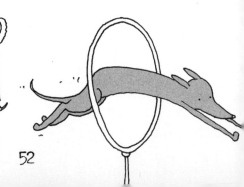

Brittney caught Fizz's leg as he stepped onto the arena. "Have a nice trip," she said. He tripped and skidded across the floor in a rolling ball of bows and curls, coming to a messy stop right in front the judges.

Brittney smiled with satisfaction.

"He's blown it," howled Amadeus from the stage stairs. A nervous whisper rippled through the crowd.

Fizz needed a talent and fast. He looked around the arena, searching for inspiration. Suddenly he saw it: a Maltese mother soothing her crying puppy with a lullaby. In a flash, Fizz knew what to do. He *did* have a talent – a talent for puppy soothing. He stood tall, took a long deep breath and sang.

His voice was sweet and smooth, and floated across the arena like a lullaby to a baby. Fizz sang like an angel!

The crowd hushed.

"Simply breathtaking!" said Miss Sparkles, dramatically wiping a tear from her eye. "It's a score of ten from the judges."

"That's *my* boy!" squealed Fizz's mother. "My Angel's a top six finalist!"

Chapter 8

The Arrest

"**T**his is it!" whispered Fizz, tingling all over as Miss Sparkles escorted the top six finalists past the guard dogs onto the stage. "We've got to catch Brittney when she steals the tiara. This is our only chance. Blow it and we'll fail our first case!"

Fizz and Remi stood on the stage, along with Brittney, Jemarcus and two other winning show dogs. In front of them, glittering on its pedestal, sat the priceless Pemberley Tiara.

Fizz took a calming breath and looked out at the gathering crowd. Sergeant Stern had arrived with two junior officers, ready for an arrest. Benny bounced on the spot, and Amadeus was at the stage stairs with Razor, ready for action.

"I'll watch Brittney," said Fizz. "You keep a close eye on her mother. She'll be the one causing the diversion."

Remi nodded.

Fizz ran through the jewel thief clues in his head: the white hair, the glass bead, the emerald jewel and the accomplice. The clues pointed to Brittney and her mother. All he had to do was catch Brittney red-handed with the tiara while her mother distracted everyone's attention.

Miss Sparkles was holding the runner-up sashes in her hand. She introduced each finalist. Brittney made a charming curtsy, and Jemarcus swished his dreads so they swept the floor. Fizz, Remi and the other two finalists each bowed and curtsied in turn.

Fizz looked down the line of finalists as the spotlight swept the stage. Something caught his eye. Jemarcus's emerald medallion sparkled beautifully in the spotlight, all except the center where an emerald was missing! And what's more, Jemarcus's chin wasn't clean, it was stained with gravy!

Fizz panicked. He ran through the clues again: the white hair, the glass bead, the emerald jewel, the accomplice and the missing talcum powder.

"The missing talcum powder!" gasped Fizz. "Remi, we forgot about the missing talcum powder! Not all the clues fit. We've got the wrong dog – the jewel thief isn't Brittney, it's Jemarcus! Look!"

Remi studied Jemarcus as the spotlight swept the stage again.

"The emerald jewel in my costume bag was from Jemarcus's medallion, not Brittney's tiara," explained Fizz. "Jemarcus has white hair and glass beads in his dreadlocks. The bead belongs to Jemarcus, not Brittney's mother. And we forgot about the missing talcum powder. A komondor isn't called a mop dog for nothing. He would sweep up any powder with his coat! We were going to arrest the wrong dog!"

"But it can't be Jemarcus," said Remi, watching Brittney's mother as she pushed her way to the front of the crowd. "The jewel thief has an accomplice. Jemarcus can't be in two places at once!"

"He can if he has a twin," said Fizz. "Miss Sparkles said Jemarcus was retiring to travel the world with his *twin* brother. Jemarcus isn't alone – his brother is here! I think they're stealing the tiaras to pay for their world trip."

"So Benny's not seeing things," said Remi. "He saw Jemarcus at the registration table *and* at the canteen eating bacon."

"Or his twin brother. It could have been either," nodded Fizz. "Oh no! The bacon! Benny said the electrical mains closet smelled of bacon. They're going to cut the lights."

Fizz searched for Benny in the crowd.

"Benny!" yelled Fizz from the stage. "Quick!"

It was too late. In that instant the lights went out and the Pemberley Show Dog Hall fell into darkness!

Brittney screamed.

Miss Sparkles yelled for help.

The tiara pedestal crashed to the ground.

"He's stealing the tiara!" cried Fizz.

"I can't see anything, where is he?" said Remi. "We're going to fail our first case, Fizz."

"We can't see, but we can smell and we can hear. Remi, follow the smell of bacon and the clack of beads," said Fizz.

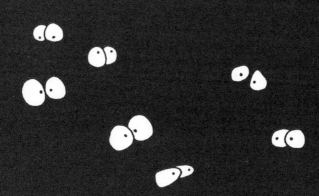

Fizz and Remi pursued the scent of bacon and the sound of beads across the stage, then leapt into the darkness. Fizz landed heavily upon the back of a dog, and felt Remi land right beside him. The dog underneath him crashed to the floor. Fizz hoped they'd captured the jewel thief.

crash

Suddenly the lights came on.

"Get those brutes off my Brittney!" cried Brittney's mother.

Fizz could hardly bear to look. If he was on top of Brittney then they'd jumped on the wrong dog and the real jewel thief would have gotten away.

He looked down. Underneath him was a flattened komondor with the Pemberley Tiara wedged firmly in his mouth.

"We got him! It's the twin brother!" cheered Remi.

"Let her go, you big brutes!" barked Brittney's mother. Amadeus and Razor were holding Brittney. They'd arrested the wrong dog!

"No you don't!" cried Fizz, wobbling as Jemarcus's brother staggered to his feet. "Remi, we're not heavy enough. He's going to get away. Amadeus, help!"

Amadeus raced across the stage. He leapt onto the back of the enormous komondor and pinned him to the stage floor.

"Thanks, Amadeus," said Fizz.

"Not bad detective work," said Amadeus, "for a little, fluffy dog."

Fizz and Remi wagged their tails together.

Sergeant Stern raced onto the scene. "Great teamwork," he said, taking the Pemberley Tiara from the komondor's mouth. "That will be the last tiara you ever steal!"

Benny grabbed Jemarcus by the light switches and escorted him to Sergeant Stern.

"I found this," said Benny.

Benny parted Jemarcus's dreadlocks with his nose. Tucked under his coat was the stolen diamond collar.

"Your father's collar," cried Fizz's mother.

"They've been smuggling the jewels out in their coats," said Benny. "No wonder the police never found anything during the bag search."

"That's why Jemarcus's coat sparkled in the Talent Quest," said Remi. "It really was diamonds."

Two police officers marched Jemarcus and his twin brother out of the hall and into the back of a paddy wagon.

"Congratulations, everyone," said Sergeant Stern. "You caught the Show Dog Jewel Thieves and solved your first case."

Fizz barked proudly, Remi pirouetted in excitement and Amadeus let out a glorious howl.

Miss Sparkles stepped up to her microphone with the Pemberley Tiara in one hand and the runner-up sashes in the other.

"I do have an awards ceremony to finish," she said, quieting the crowd with a brilliant smile. "The winner of the Pemberley Show Dog Trials and this year's recipient of the Pemberley Tiara is… Angel."

Fizz's mother yelped with delight.

Brittney stormed off the stage.

Miss Sparkles sat the glittering Pemberley Tiara on Fizz's head. Then she placed a runner-up sash around Remi and Benny. "For bravery," she said.

Amadeus burst out laughing. "Sweet! Go, Powder Puff!"

"Oh, I haven't forgotten you," said Miss Sparkles, placing a runner-up sash around Amadeus's neck. "You were very brave too."

Amadeus flexed his muscles in a show dog pose.

"In fact," continued Miss Sparkles, admiring Amadeus's midnight black coat, "you could be a show dog champion, too, with fur like that."

"What?!" said Amadeus.

Fizz, Remi and Benny cheered.

"I'd like to keep both my boys, Miss Sparkles," said Sergeant Stern. "I wouldn't want to break up a winning team."

Amadeus nodded.

"Whoo-hoo!" sang Fizz, tingling all over with happiness.

The story continues in **Book 4**

FIZZ and the HANDBAG DOGNAPPER

From the Author and the Illustrator

When Lesley Gibbes discovered that her father-in-law's childhood nickname was "Fizz," she knew it was the perfect name for her fluffy undercover police dog. But it was her two naughty Jack Russell terriers, Porsche and Cosworth, who were the real inspiration for Fizz. Just like Fizz, they're clever, brave and fast. And even though they are only the size of a tomcat, they both think they're as big and as bold as a German shepherd.

When Stephen Michael King was a boy he liked to draw dogs: dogs scuba diving, driving cars, playing guitar or flying into outer space... anything he could imagine a normal dog doing on any normal day. Now Stephen is married with two grown children, one parrot and three dogs, and he still finds himself drawing dogs: dogs in cars, on motorbikes, dressed in silly costumes and chasing robbers.